# THE BLACK MADONNA

## AND OTHER STORIES

D1675189

DORIS LESSING

# THE BLACK MADONNA

## AND OTHER STORIES

The vocabulary is based on
Michael West: A General Service List of
English Words, revised & enlarged edition 1953
Pacemaker Core Vocabulary, 1975
Salling/Hvid: English-Danish Basic Dictionary, 1970
J. A. van Ek: The Threshold Level for Modern Language
Learning in Schools, 1976

Editor: Solveig Odland

Illustrations: Oskar Jørgensen

Cover layout: Mette Plesner
Cover illustration: Pawel Marczak

*The De Wets Come to Kloof Grange*, taken from
THIS WAS THE OLD CHIEF'S COUNTRY
by Doris Lessing, first published in Great Britain
by Michael Joseph Ltd., 1973.

*The Black Madonna and The Words He Said*, taken from
THE SUN BETWEEN THEIR FEET by Doris Lessing,
first published in Great Britain by Michael Joseph Ltd., 1973.

© 1980 by ASCHEHOUG A/S
for the Easy Reader - edition
ISBN Denmark 87-11-09162-2

Printed in Denmark by
Sangill Grafisk Produktion, Holme Olstrup

## DORIS LESSING

was born in Iran in 1919. In 1924 the family went to farm in Rhodesia (now Zimbabwe), where Doris Lessing spent a solitary childhood, reading and walking through the African bush. She came to Britain in 1949 and has lived there ever since as a professional writer.

The accumulated experience of Doris Lessing's Rhodesian years was crystallized in her first two published books: »The Grass is Singing« (1950), a novel, and »This Was the Old Chief's Country« (1951), a volume of short stories.

This first novel introduces two of Doris Lessing's principal themes – the misuse of blacks by whites in Africa, and the equally destructive conflict between men and women everywhere.

The stories collected in »Five« received the 1953 Somerset Maugham Award.

In 1962 »The Golden Notebook« appeared. Meanwhile Doris Lessing had begun to publish the very long novel »Children of Violence«, which appeared in five volumes between 1952 and 1969. »Martha Quest« (1952), »A Proper Marriage« (1954), »A Ripple From the Storm« (1958), »Landlocked« (1965), »The Four-Gated City« (1969). Other novels are »Briefing for a Descent Into Hell« (1971), »The Summer Before the Dark« (1973) and »Memoires of a Survivor« (1974).

»Going Home« (1957) is a collection of essays about the authoress' return visit to Africa in the mid 1950s. For the theatre she has written »Each His Own Wilderness« (1959), »Play With a Tiger« (1962).

»The Sirian Experiments« (1980) is the third book in Doris Lessing's space age saga »Canopus in Argos: Archives«, which she began in »Shikasta« and continued in »The Marriage Between Zones Three, Four, and Five«. The fourth will be »The Making of Representative for Planet 8«.

# CONTENTS

# The De Wets come to Kloof *Grange*

*nass, feucht.*

veranda

pillars

The *veranda,* which was lifted on stone *pillars,* hung
over the garden like a box in the theatre. Below were *unter*
*luxuriant* masses of flowering bushes. A splendid *herrlich*
sunset filled the sky with bright red, *purple* and
applegreen, fading gently into a wide stretch of grey, *strecken*
blown over by slightly coloured clouds. And in this
still evening sky hung a small clear moon.

There sat Major Gale and his wife, as they did every
evening at this hour, nicely side by side, critically *kritisch*
watching this splendid sight presented for them.

Major Gale said, with satisfaction, "Good sunset *zufrieden*
tonight," and they both turned their eyes to the moon.
The *dusk* drew veils across sky and garden. Mrs Gale *verschließen*
rose, folded her chair and put it up against the wall. *zusammen-*
*falten*

---

*grange,* a country house with farm buildings.
*luxuriant,* having very great growth of leaves, branches etc.
*purple,* a dark colour formed by the mixture of blue and red.
*dusk,* the faint light at the end of the day.

koodoo horns

"Here comes the post," she said. Major Gale went to the steps, waiting for the native who, filled with <u>fear</u> of the dark, was <u>hastening towards them</u> through the <u>tall</u> shadowing bushes. He swung a sack from his back and handed it to Major Gale. Then he ran around the corner of the house to the back, where there were lights and companions.

*hastening towards them = sich beeilen zu ihm zu kommen.*

rug

Mrs Gale lifted the sack and went into the front room. There she lit the oil lamp and sorted the letters into two piles. Then husband and wife sat themselves down opposite each other to read their mail.

It was more than an ordinary farm living room. There were *koodoo horns* branching out over the fire-place, but on the floor were fine *rugs,* and the furniture

9

was two hundred years old. The table was <u>polished</u> by Mrs Gale herself every day before she set on it an *earthenware* pot with red flowers. Africa and the English eighteenth century *mingled* in this room and were at peace.

From time to time Mrs Gale rose to <u>attend</u> to the lamp, which did not burn well. Above the heads of the Gales a cloud of flying <u>insects</u> <u>sought</u> their death in its light and <u>dropped</u> one by one, plop, plop, plop to the table <u>among</u> the letters.

Mrs Gale took an <u>envelope</u> from her own pile and handed it to her husband. "A letter from the assistant," she remarked, her eyes bent on her own mail. She smiled tenderly as she read. The letter was from her oldest friend, a woman doctor in London. They had written to each other every week for thirty years, ever since Mrs Gale came to *exile* in Southern Rhodesia. She said half-aloud, "Why, Betty's brother's

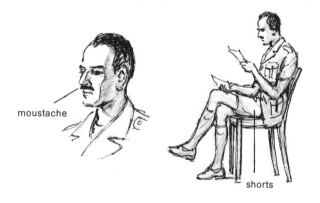

moustache

shorts

---

*earthenware,* pots, dishes etc. made of baked clay.
*mingle,* mix.
*exile,* a long stay in a foreign land.

daughter is going to study law," and though she had never met Betty's brother, let alone the daughter, the news seemed to please and excite her extraordinarily. The whole of the letter was about people she had never met and was not likely ever to meet – about the weather, about English politics. Indeed, there was not a sentence in it that would not have struck an outsider as having been written out of a sense of duty. But when Mrs Gale had finished reading it, she put it aside gently and sat smiling quietly. She had gone back half a century to her *childhood*.

Gradually sight returned to her eyes, and she saw her husband where before she had sat looking through him. He appeared disturbed. There was something wrong about the letter from the assistant.

Major Gale was a tall and still *military* figure, even in his *khaki* shirt and *shorts*. He changed them twice a day. The *creases* in his shorts were sharp as folded paper, and the pockets of his shirt were always buttoned up tight. His small head, with its polished surface of black hair, his little black *moustache,* his farmer's hands with their broken but clean nails – all these seemed to say that it was no easy matter not to let oneself go, not to let this *damned* easy-going country get under one's skin. It wasn't easy, but he did it. One finds a man like Major Gale only in exile.

He rose from his chair and began walking back and forth, while his wife watched him and waited for him

---

*childhood,* the time of being a child.
*military,* of, for soldiers; here, soldier-like.
*khaki,* a greenish-brown colour; also cloth of this colour.
*crease,* a mark or line made by a fold.
*damn,* to sentence to unending punishment in hell; here a curse.

to tell her what was the matter. At last he sighed, with a glance at her, and when she said, "Well, dear?" he replied at once, "The man has a wife."

"Dear me!" she exclaimed.

At once as if he had been waiting for her protest, he returned *briskly,* "It will be nice for you to have another woman about the place."

"Yes, I suppose it will," she said *humorously.* At this most familiar note in her voice, he looked up and said sharply, "You always complain I bury you alive."

And so she did, but not so often now. In fact, she had learned to love her *isolation,* and she felt sad that he did not know it.

"But they can't come to the house. That I really couldn't put up with." The plan had been for the new assistant – Major Gale's farm had become too successful for him to manage any longer by himself – to have the spare room, and share the house with his employers.

"No, I suppose not, if there's a wife." Major Gale sounded doubtful. It was clear he would not mind another family sharing with them. "Perhaps they could have the old house?" he asked at last.

"I'll see to it," said Mrs Gale, removing the weight of worry off her husband's shoulders. Things he could manage, but people bothered him. That they bothered her, too, now, was something he didn't understand. She knew he was hardly conscious of her. Nothing existed for him outside his farm. And this suited her

*brisk,* lively, active.
*humorous,* amusing, gay; funny.
*isolation,* the state of being alone or separated from others.

12

well. Now, with the four children grown up, they were friends and could forget each other. What a relief when he no longer 'loved' her! (That was how she put it.) Growing old had its advantages.

When she said, "I'll see to it," he glanced at her, suddenly, directly. Her tone had been a little too comforting. He really observed her for a moment. He saw an *elderly* Englishwoman, thin and dry, sitting calmly over her letters, looking at him with her small blue eyes. A guilty look in them troubled him. He crossed to her and kissed her cheek. "There!" he said, leaning forward with a lively laugh. Confused he stopped for a moment, then said with determination, "I shall go and have my bath." *Entschlossenheit*

After his bath they ate their dinner. Immediately the meal was over he said, "Bed," and moved off. He was always in bed before eight and up by five. Once Mrs Gale had followed her husband's habit. Now, with their four boys out sailing the seven seas in the *navy,* and nothing really to get her out of bed, she slept until eight, when she joined her husband for breakfast. So, when her husband had gone to bed she remained under the lamp, reading or simply dreaming about the past, the very distant past, when she had been Caroline Morgan, living near a small country town, a country gentleman's daughter. That was how she liked best to think of herself.

Tonight she soon turned down the lamp and stepped on to the veranda. Now the moon was a large, soft, yellow fruit caught in the top branches of a tree.

---

*elderly,* nearing old age.
*navy,* a nation's battleships.

She passed quietly down the steps and beneath the trees, with one quick glance back at the bedroom window. Her husband hated her to be out of the house by herself at night.

She was on her way to the old house that lay half a mile away over the *veld*.

Before the Gales had come to this farm, two South African brothers had it. The first thing she did on arriving was to change the name of the farm from Kloof Nek to Kloof Grange, to remind her of home. One of the houses was emptied of furniture and used for storing things. It was a square, bare box of a place, stuck in the middle of the bare veld, and its shut windows flashed back light to the sun all day. But her own home had been added to, and surrounded with verandas and fenced off. Inside the fence there was a large garden that she had *created* over years of hard work. And what a garden! She lived for her flowering

---

*veld,* in South Africa, open country with grass and few or no trees.

*create,* to bring into being.

African *shrubs,* her English *lawns,* her water-garden with *goldfish* and *water-lilies.* Not many people had such a garden.

She walked through it this evening under the moon, feeling herself grow lightheaded with the influence of the strange greenish light, and of the smell of the flowers. She touched the leaves with her fingers as she passed, bending her face to the roses. She paused at the gate, looking over the space of empty veld between her and the other house. She did not like going outside her garden at night. She was not afraid of the natives, no. She regarded Africans as rather *pathetic* children, and

---

*shrub,* a low bush.
*lawn,* area of smooth grass in a garden.
*goldfish,* a kind of golden-yellow fish, often kept as a pet.
*water-lily,* a type of plant growing in lakes etc. with flat floating leaves and large flowers.
*pathetic,* causing pity.

was very kind to them. She did not know what made her afraid. So she took a deep breath, and stepped carefully through the gate, shutting it behind her. The road before her was a white strip of sand. On either side were short and thick trees, and their shadows were deep and black. Why, this was only the road she walked along every afternoon. Slowing her steps, as a discipline, she moved through the pools of shadow, feeling relief each time she stepped into the moonlight. Finally she came to the house. It looked dead, a dead thing with staring eyes. *Nonsense,* she told herself. Nonsense. She walked to the front door, unlocked it, and flashed her *torch* over the floor. Sacks of grain were piled to the ceiling and mice ran quickly to safety. She drew in a deep breath and made a list in her head of what had to be done. She was a very *capable* woman.

Then something struck her. If the man had forgotten, when applying for the job, to mention a wife, he was quite likely to forget children too. If they had children it wouldn't do, no it wouldn't do. She simply couldn't put up with a tribe of children – for *Afrikaners* never had less than twelve – running wild over the beautiful garden. Anger filled her. De Wet – the name was hard on her tongue. Her husband should not have agreed to take on an Afrikaner. Really, really,

torch

---

*nonsense,* words or ideas that have no meaning.
*capable,* here, able to deal with difficulties without help.
*Afrikaner,* native of South Africa, of European, esp. Dutch origin.

Caroline, she said to herself, standing there in the deserted house, don't be unfair.

She decided to arrange the house for a man and his wife, without considering any children. She would arrange things, in kindness, for a woman who might not be used to living in *loneliness*. But when she tried to form a picture of this woman who was coming to share her life, imagination failed her. She pictured a large, *homely* Dutch woman, and was *repulsed*. For the first time the knowledge that she must soon, next week, take another woman into her life, came home to her, and she *disliked* it strongly.

Why must she? Her husband would not have to make a friend of the man. They would work together, that was all. But because they, the wives, were two women on an *isolated* farm, they would be expected to live in each other's pockets. She strongly opposed it. She had put a distance between herself and other people, even her own husband. And because she opposed the idea, she began to think of her friend Betty, as if it were she who would be coming to the farm.

Still thinking of her friend Betty she returned through the silent veld, imagining them walking together over this road and talking as they had been used to. You are a silly woman, Caroline, she said to herself. Three years before they had gone on holiday to England, and she had found she and Betty had

---

*loneliness,* the state of being lonely.
*homely,* plain but pleasant.
*repulsed,* put off by something you do not like.
*dislike,* to not like.
*isolated,* lonely.

nothing to say to each other. Their lives were so far apart, and had been for so long. Their friendship had died years before. She knew it very well, but tried not to think of it. In her loneliness it was necessary for her to have Betty remain, in imagination at least.

The next day, and the days following, she cleaned and swept and tidied the old house, not for Mrs De Wet, but for Betty. Otherwise she could not have gone through with it. When it was all finished she walked through the rooms which she had furnished with things taken from her own home, and said to a *visionary* Betty (but Betty as she had been thirty years before), "Well, what do you think of it?" The place was bare but clean now, and smelling of sunlight and air, and there were flowers everywhere. "You would like living here," Mrs Gale said to Betty, before locking the house up and returning to her own, feeling as if she had won a victory over herself.

The De Wets sent a *wire* saying they would arrive on Sunday after lunch. That would spoil her rest, for she slept every day through the afternoon heat. Major Gale, for whom every day was a working day, went off to a distant part of the farm to look at his cattle. Mrs Gale laid herself down on her bed with her eyes shut and listened for a car. She slept uncomfortably, fighting all afternoon with the knowledge that she should stay awake. When she woke at four she was angry and tired, and there was still no sign of a car.

She rose and dressed herself. Then she left a message

---

*visionary,* seen in imagination only.
*wire,* message send by telegraph.

leopard

crocodile

with the houseboy that she would be in the garden and walked away from the veranda with a strong excitement growing in her. This excitement rose as she moved through the crowding shrubs under the walls, through the rose garden with its wide green lawns that were watered all year round, and arrived at her favourite spot among the *fountains* and the pools of water-lilies.

She sat herself on a shaded bench. On one side were the fountains, the roses, the lawns, the house, and beyond them the wind-bitten high veld. On the other, the ground dropped hundreds of feet sharply to the river. She would sit here for hours, on her *rocky* shelf, leaning outwards, her short grey hair blown across her face, lost in worship of the hills across the river. Not of the river itself, no, she thought of that with a sense of danger, for there, below her, in that dirty green water, were *crocodiles,* and *leopards* came from the rocks to drink. Sitting there on her shelf, a smell of sunwarmed green, of hot decaying water, of luxuriant growth, rose in waves to her face. She had learned to *ignore* it and to ignore the river while she watched the hills. They were h e r hills, that was how she felt. For years she had sat here hours every day watching the cloud shadows move over them, watching them turn blue with distance or come close after rain. They were never the same half an hour together. They were her mountains, they were what she was, they had made her, had turned her loneliness into strength.

*fountain,* see picture, page 33.
*rocky,* of rock.
*crocodile, leopard,* see picture, page 19.
*ignore,* to take no notice of.

And now she almost forgot the De Wets were coming, and were hours late. Almost, not quite. At last, realizing that the sun was setting, she began to worry. Something might have happened to them? They had taken the wrong road, perhaps? Their car had broken down? And the Major was miles away in their own car, so there was no way of looking for them.

Caroline, she said to herself severely, don't let things worry you so. She stood up and shook herself and pushed the hair out of her face. She stepped backwards away from the wind, sighed a good-bye to her garden for that day, and returned to the house. There, outside the front door, was a car, old and broken down, loaded with luggage, its back doors tied with rope. And children! She could see a half-grown girl on the steps. No, really, it was too much. On the other side of the car stood a tall, thin, fairheaded man, burnt a dark brown, looking for someone to come. He must be the father. She approached, arranging her face in a smile, looking *apprehensively* about her for the children. The man slowly came forward, the girl after him. "I expected you earlier," began Mrs Gale briskly. "Is Major Gale about?" he asked, and seemed not to take her into account. "I am Mrs Gale," she replied. Then again, "I expected you earlier." Really, four hours late, and not a word of excuse!

"We started late," he remarked. "Where can I put our things?"

Mrs Gale said, "I didn't know you had a family. I didn't make any arrangements."

---

*apprehensively,* with fear.

"I wrote to the Major about my wife," said De Wet. "Didn't he get my letter?" He sounded angry.

Weakly Mrs Gale said, "Your wife?" and looked astonished at the girl, who was smiling *awkwardly* behind her husband. It could be seen, looking at her more closely, that she might perhaps be eighteen. She was a small creature, with delicate brown legs and arms, a brush of dancing black curls, and large excited black eyes. She put both hands round her husband's arm, and said, *giggling,* "I am Mrs De Wet. We got married last week."

"Last week," said Mrs Gale, with a sense of dislike.

The girl said, half bold, half *shy,* "He met me in the

---

*awkward,* uncomfortable.
*giggle,* to laugh in a nervous or silly way.
*shy,* lacking confidence in the presence of others.

cinema and we got married next day." It seemed as if she were in some way offering herself to the older woman, offering something precious of herself.

"Really," said Mrs Gale politely, glancing almost apprehensively at this man, this slow-moving, clever South African, who had behaved so madly. Dislike twisted her again. Suddenly the man took the girl by the arm and shaking her gently said, "Thought I had better get myself a wife to cook for me, all this way out in the blue. No restaurants, here, hey, Doodle?"

"Oh, Jack," said the girl, giggling. "All he thinks about is his stomach," she said to Mrs Gale, as one girl to another, and then glanced with *delicious* fear at her husband.

"Cooking is what I married you for," he said, smiling down at her.

There stood Mrs Gale opposite them, and she saw that they had forgotten her presence, and that it was only with the greatest effort of will that they did not kiss. "Well," she remarked dryly, "this is a surprise."

They fell apart, their faces changing. They became at once what they had been during the first moments: two *hostile* strangers. They looked at her and saw a middle-aged English lady, smiling at them coldly with narrow critical eyes.

"I'll take you to your house," she said. "I'll walk, and you go in the car – no, I walk it often." Nothing in the world would make her get into that car.

She marched stiffly before them along the road and

*delicious,* giving pleasure.
*hostile,* not friendly.

the car followed her slowly. She knew it was *ridiculous,* she could feel their eyes on her back, but she could not help it.

When they reached the house, she unlocked it, showed them what arrangements had been made, and left them. She walked back filled with anger, caused mostly because of her picture of herself walking along the same road, followed by the car, and refusing to do the only reasonable thing, which was to get into it with them.

She sat on her veranda for half an hour, looking at the sunset sky without seeing it. Then she called the houseboy, and gave him a note, asking the two to come to dinner. No sooner had the boy left than she called him back. "I'll go myself," she said. This was partly to prove that she made nothing of walking the half mile, and partly because she was sorry about the way she had behaved. After all, it was no crime to get married, and they seemed very fond of each other. That was how she put it.

When she came to the house, the front room was filled with luggage, paper, pots and *pans.* All the beautiful order she had created was destroyed. She could hear voices from the bedroom.

"But, Jack, I don't want you to. I want you to stay with me." And then his voice, humorous, proud, slow, *amorous,* "You'll do what I tell you, my girl. I've got to see the old man. I start work tomorrow, don't forget."

---

*ridiculous,* very silly.
*pan,* a low, broad pot or vessel used in cooking.
*amorous,* loving.

"But, Jack . . ." There came sounds of struggling and laughter.

"Well," said Mrs Gale, drawing in her breath. She knocked on the wood of the door and all sound stopped. "Come in," came the girl's voice. Mrs Gale hesitated, then went into the bedroom.

Mrs De Wet was sitting on the bed, combing her hair. Mrs Gale noted that the two beds had already been pushed together. "I've come to ask you to dinner," she said briskly. "You don't want to have to cook when you've just come."

"Oh no, don't trouble, Mrs Gale," said De Wet awkwardly. "We'll get ourselves something, don't worry." He glanced at the girl and said, "She'll get busy with the tin-opener in a minute, I expect. That's her idea of feeding a man."

"Oh, Jack," said his wife.

"Thanks all the same," continued De Wet. "But tell the Major I'll be over after dinner to talk things over."

"Very well," said Mrs Gale, "just as you like."

She walked away from the house. Now she felt *rebuffed*. After all, they might have been so polite as to come. Yet she was pleased they hadn't. If they preferred making love to getting to know the people who were to be their neighbours for what might be years, it was their own affair . . .

Mrs De Wet was saying, as she painted her toenails, with her knees drawn up to her chin, "Who the hell does she think she is anyway? Surely she could give us

---

*rebuffed,* not accepted.

a meal without *making* such a *fuss* when we've just
come."

"She came to ask us, didn't she?"

"Hoping we would say no."

Mrs Gale knew quite well that this was what they
were thinking, and felt it was unjust. She would have
liked them to come. The man wasn't a bad sort, in his
way, a simple soul, but pleasant enough. As for the
girl, she would have to learn, that was all. But in spite
of that she knew that if she had behaved differently
they would have come. She was angry during dinner,
and the meal was not half finished when there was a
knock on the door. De Wet stood there.

Major Gale left the table and went out to the

---

*make fuss,* to worry or cause trouble about small matters.

veranda to discuss business. Mrs Gale finished her dinner, and then joined the two men. Her husband rose politely at her coming, offered her a chair, sat down and forgot her presence. She listened to them talking for some two hours, then she went indoors.

As she went to bed, she felt tired, because of her broken sleep that afternoon. But she could not sleep then, either. She listened to the sound of the men's voices. They seemed to be enjoying themselves. It was after twelve when she heard De Wet say, in that slow humorous way of his, "I'd better be getting home. I'll catch it hot, as it is." And, with *rage,* Mrs Gale heard her husband laugh. He actually laughed. She realized that she herself had been planning a sharp remark for when he came to the bedroom. So when he did enter, smelling of tobacco smoke, and grinning, and then walked about the room in his underclothes, she said nothing, but noted that he was getting fat, in spite of all the hard work he did.

"Well, what do you think of the man?"

"He'll do well indeed," said Major Gale, with satisfaction. "He knows his stuff all right. He's been doing mixed farming in the Transvaal* for years." After a moment he asked politely, as he got into his own bed on the other side of the room, "And what is she like?"

"I haven't seen much of her, have I? But she seems pleasant enough."

"Someone for you to talk to," said Major Gale, turning himself over to sleep. "You had better ask her over to tea."

---

*rage,* great anger.
*Part of the Republic of South Africa.

At this Mrs Gale sat straight up in her own bed. Someone for her to talk to, indeed! But she composed herself, said good night in her usual rather brisk way, and lay awake. Next day she must certainly ask the girl to morning tea. It would be rude not to. Besides, that would leave the afternoon free for her garden and her mountains.

Next morning she sent a boy across with a note. She went herself to the kitchen to bake some cakes. At eleven o'clock she was seated on the veranda.

At last she heard footsteps up the path. There was the girl, preparing her face for a social occasion, walking *primly* through the *bougainvillea* arches, in a flowered dress just as colourful as her surroundings. Mrs Gale jumped to her feet and cried gaily, "I am so glad you had time to come." Mrs De Wet giggled and said, "But I had nothing else to do, had I?"

Afterwards she said angrily to her husband, "She's crazy. She sends me letters in closed envelopes when I'm five minutes away, and says Have I the time? What the hell else did she think I had to do?" And then, violently, "She can't have anything to do. There was enough food to feed ten."

"Wouldn't be a bad idea if you spent more time cooking," said De Wet fondly.

The next day Mrs Gale worked in her garden, feeling guilty all the time, because she could not bring

---

*prim,* very correct.
*bougainvillea,* plant with bright-coloured leaves.

herself to send over another note of invitation.

After a few days, she invited the De Wets to dinner. Throughout the meal she made polite conversation with the girl while the men lost themselves in cattle diseases. What could one talk to a girl like that about? Nothing! Mrs De Wet was not interested in cooking, and when Mrs Gale gave advice about ordering clothes from England, which was so much cheaper than buying them in the local towns, the reply came that she had made all her own clothes since she was seven. After that there seemed nothing to say, for it was hardly possible to remark that these bright sundresses were quite *unsuitable* for the farm, besides being foolish, since bare shoulders in this sun were dangerous.

There were two more tea parties, then they were allowed to stop. From time to time Mrs Gale wondered, what the poor girl did with herself all day, and felt it was her duty to go and find out. But she did not.

One morning the houseboy came and said the little *missus* was on the veranda and she was sick.

Mrs Gale almost ran to the veranda. There was the girl, sitting in a chair, her face *contorted,* her eyes red, her whole body trembling violently. *"Malaria,"* thought Mrs Gale at once, noting that trembling.

"What is the trouble, my dear?" Her voice was kind.

---

*unsuitable,* not convenient.
*missus,* little madam (native slang).
*contorted,* twisted out of shape.
*malaria,* a disease.

She put her hand on the girl's shoulder. Mrs De Wet turned and threw her arms around her, *weeping,* weeping, her small head buried in Mrs Gale's stomach. Holding herself stiffly away from this unpleasant contact, Mrs Gale stroked the girl's head.

"Mrs Gale, Mrs Gale . . ."

"What is it?"

"I can't stand it. I shall go mad, I simply can't stand it."

Mrs Gale, seeing that the girl was not ill, lifted her up, led her inside, and laid her on her own bed. After a while Mrs De Wet grew silent. Finally she sat up with a little smile and said pathetically, "I am a fool."

"But what is it, dear?"

"It isn't anything really. I am so lonely. I wanted to get my mother up to stay with me, only Jack said there wasn't room, and he's quite right, only I got mad, because I thought he might at least have had my mother. . ."

Mrs Gale felt guilty, she could have filled the place of this child's mother.

"And it isn't anything, Mrs Gale, not really. It's not that I'm not happy with Jack. I am, but I never see him. I'm not used to this kind of thing. I come from a family of thirteen counting my parents, and I simply can't stand it."

Mrs Gale sat and listened, and thought of her own loneliness when she first began this sort of life.

"He comes in late, not till seven sometimes. I know he can't help it, with his farm work and all that, and then he has supper and goes straight off to bed. I

---

*weep,* to cry tears.

am not sleepy then. I get up sometimes and walk along the road with my dog . . ."

Mrs Gale thought, This girl should have a baby; and could not help glancing at her stomach.

Mrs De Wet, who missed nothing, said *resentfully,* "Jack says I should have a baby. That's all he says." She changed at once from a crying baby to a hostile young woman with whom Mrs Gale could have no contact. "I'm sorry," she said formally. Then, with a smile, "Thank you for letting me blow off steam." She climbed off the bed and shook her skirts straight. Then she added, "So that's how it goes. Who would be a woman, eh?"

Mrs Gale *stiffened.* "You must come and see me whenever you are lonely," she said, equally bright and false. She couldn't understand how this girl could come to her with all her defences down, and then suddenly shut her out with this nonsense. But she felt more comfortable with the distance between them.

"Oh, I will, Mrs Gale. Thank you ever so much for asking me." Mrs Gale watched the girl walking gaily through the gate. Letting off steam! Well, she said to herself, well . . . And she went back to her garden.

That afternoon she made a point of walking across to the other house. She would offer to show Mrs De Wet the garden. The two women returned together, Mrs Gale wondering if the girl regretted her behaviour in the morning. If so, she showed no signs of it.

They passed the house through the shrubs. There were the fountains, sending up their showers of water,

---

*resentful,* angry, bitter.
*stiffen,* to become stiff.

the cool water-lilies, under which coloured fish slipped.

"This must cost a lot to keep up," said Mrs De Wet. She stood at the edge of the pool, looking at her reflection among the broad green leaves, glanced up at Mrs Gale, and *dabbed* her red toenails in the water.

Mrs Gale saw that she was thinking of herself as her husband's employer's wife. "It does rather," she said dryly, remembering that the only quarrels she ever had with her husband were over the cost of *pumping* water. "You are fond of gardens?" she asked. She could not imagine anyone not being fond of gardens.

Mrs De Wet said resentfully, "My mother was always too busy having kids to have time for a garden. She had her last baby early this year." Mrs Gale, seeing that all this beauty and peace meant nothing to her companion, said, playing her last card, "Come and see my mountains."

When she had the girl safely on the rocky edge of the steep bank, she heard her say, "There's my river." She was leaning forward over the great *gulf,* and her voice was lifted with excitement. "Look," she was saying, "look, there it is." She turned to Mrs Gale, laughing.

"Mind, you'll lose your balance." Mrs Gale pulled her back. "You have been down to the river, then?"

"I go there every morning."

Mrs Gale was silent. How could that be possible? "But it is four miles there and four back."

"Oh, I'm used to walking."

---

*dab,* to strike lightly.
*pump,* to raise water by machine.
*gulf,* here, a drop between high rocks.

fountain

"But . . ." Mrs Gale heard her own unpleasant voice and stopped herself. There was after all no reason why the girl should not go to the river. "What do you do there?"

"I sit on the edge of a big rock with my legs in the water, and I fish sometimes. And I pick up water-lilies."

"There are crocodiles," said Mrs Gale sharply. The girl was mad. Anyone was who could like that unpleasant place with its heat and smells. "A native girl was taken last year."

"There couldn't be a crocodile where I go. The water is clear, right down. You can see right under the rocks. It is a lovely pool. There are water-birds, all colours. They are so pretty. And when you sit there and look, the sky is a long narrow *slit*. From here it looks quite far across the river to the other side, but really it isn't. And the trees crowding close make it narrower. Just think how many millions of years it must have taken for the water to wear down the rock so deep."

"There's *bilharzia,* too."

"Oh, bilharzia!"

"There's nothing funny about bilharzia," said Mrs Gale. My husband had it. He had treatment for six months before he was cured."

The girl's face dulled. "I'll be careful," she said, turning away, holding her river and her long hot *dreamy* mornings away form Mrs Gale, like a secret.

"Let's go and have some tea," said Mrs Gale. She felt

---

*slit,* a long narrow opening.
*bilharzia,* a disease.
*dreamy,* full of dreams.

angry and put out, she had no idea why. And so at last they were quite silent together, and in silence they remained on that veranda above the beautiful garden, drinking their tea and wishing it was time for them to part.

Soon they saw the two husbands coming up the garden. Mrs De Wet's face lit up, and she sprang to her feet and was off down the path, running lightly. She caught her husband's arm and *clung* there. He put her away from him, gently. "Hullo," he said. "Eating again?" And then he turned back to Major Gale and went on talking.

On the veranda the men sank at once into chairs, took large cups of tea, and continued talking. Mrs Gale listened and smiled. Crops, cattle, disease. Weather, crop, cattle. Mrs De Wet sat on the veranda wall and swung her legs. Her lips trembled, her eyes were full of tears. Mrs Gale was saying silently under her breath, "You'll get used to it my dear, you'll get used to it." But she respected the girl, who had courage: walking to the river and back, trying to find peace – at least, she was trying to find it. She said sharply, cutting into the men's conversation, "Mr De Wet, did you know your wife spends her mornings at the river?"

The man looked at her and tried to gather the sense of her words, his mind was on the farm. "Sure," he said at last. "Why not?"

"Aren't you afraid of bilharzia?"

He said calmly, "If we were going to get it, we would

---

*cling,* to stick or hang on (to).

have got it long ago. It's too late now. Let her enjoy it."

"Mr De Wet have you ever thought what it means to a woman being alone all day, with not enough to do? It's enough to drive anyone crazy," said Mrs Gale, sharply.

"And what do you expect me to do about it?"

"You don't realize," said Mrs Gale, knowing perfectly well there was nothing he could do about it. "You don't understand how it is."

"She'll have a kid soon," said De Wet. "I hope so at any rate. That will give her something to do."

Anger raced through Mrs Gale like a flame along petrol. She was trembling. "You treat her just like she was one of your cows," she said at last.

"What's the matter with having kids?" asked De Wet. "Any objections?"

"You might ask me first," said the girl bitterly.

Her husband looked at her in surprise. "Hey, what is this?" he asked. "What have I done? You said you wanted to have kids. Wouldn't have married you otherwise."

"I never said I didn't.

"There's more to women than having children," said Mrs Gale, knowing how ridiculous she sounded.

De Wet looked her up and down, up and down. "I want kids," he said at last. "I want a large family. Make no mistake about that. And when I married her I told her I wanted them. She can't turn round now and say I didn't."

"Who is turning round and saying anything?" asked the girl, fine and proud, staring away over the trees.

"Well, if no one is blaming anyone for anything," asked Major Gale, "what is all this about?"

"God knows, I don't," said De Wet angrily. "I didn't start it."

Mrs Gale sat silent, trembling, feeling foolish, but so angry she could not speak. After a while she said to the girl, "Shall we go inside, my dear?" The girl rose and with a backward look at her husband followed Mrs Gale. "He didn't mean anything," the girl said, *apologizing* for her husband to her husband's employer's wife. At this moment, De Wet appeared in the door-

---

*apologize,* to make an excuse.

way and said, "Come on, I am going home."

"Is that an order?" asked the girl, quickly, backing so that she came side by side with Mrs Gale.

"What's got into you?" he said, angrily. "Are you coming or are you not?"

"I can't do anything else, can I?" she replied, and followed him from the house like a queen.

Major Gale came in after a few moments. "Lover's quarrel," he said, laughing awkwardly.

"That man!" she said angrily. "That man!"

"Why, what is wrong with him?" She remained silent, pretending to arrange her flowers. This silly scene made her *furious*. She was angry with herself, angry with her husband, and furious at that foolish couple who had succeeded in *upsetting* her and destroying her peace. At last she said, "I'm going to bed. I've such a headache. I can't think."

"I'll bring you a tray, my dear," said Major Gale.

"I don't want anything, thank you," she said, like a child, and marched off to the bedroom.

She went to bed and tried to read. She found she was not following the sense of the words. She put down the book, and blew out the lamp. Light streamed into the room from the moon. From next door came the sound of her husband eating his meal.

Later she heard voices from the veranda. Then her husband came into the room and said, "De Wet is asking whether his wife has been here."

"What!" exclaimed Mrs Gale, slowly understanding what this meant. "Why, has she gone off somewhere?"

---

*furious,* very angry.
   *upset,* to disturb the peace of mind of (somebody).

"She's not at home," said the Major uncomfortably. For he always became uncomfortable and very polite when he had to deal with situations like this.

"Tell that fine young man that his wife often goes for long walks by herself when he's asleep," said Mrs Gale. "He probably hasn't noticed it. Just as I used to," she could not prevent herself adding.

Major Gale gave her a look which seemed to say, "Oh lord, don't say we are going back to all that business again?" He went out, and she heard him saying, "Your wife might have gone for a walk, perhaps?" Then the young man's voice, "I know she does sometimes. I don't like her being out at night, but she just walks around the house. And she takes the dogs with her. Maybe she's gone further this time – being upset, you know."

Then they both laughed. The laughter was of a quite different quality from the responsibility of their tone a moment before, and Mrs Gale found herself sitting up in bed, saying, "How d a r e he?"

She got up and dressed herself. In the main room her husband was sitting reading, and since he seldom read, it seemed he was also worried. Neither of them spoke. When she looked at the clock, she found it was just past nine o'clock.

After an hour of anxiety, they heard the footsteps they had been waiting for. There stood De Wet, angry, worried sick, his face white, his eyes burning.

"We must get the boys out," he said, speaking directly to Major Gale, and ignoring Mrs Gale.

"I'm coming too," she said.

The three of them stood on the veranda, waiting for the natives. Everything was bathed in moonlight.

Soon they heard the growing *clamour* of voices and a little while later the darkness was lit by *torches*. Then a crowd of dark figures took shape under the broken lights. The farm natives, excited by the idea of chasing over the veld at night, were shouting and screaming as if they were after a small deer.

"Is it necessary to have all these natives in it?" asked Mrs Gale. "After all, have we even considered the possibilities? Where can a girl run to on a place like this?"

"That's a point," said Major Gale coldly.

"I can't bear to think of her being chased, like this, by a crowd of natives. It's horrible."

"More horrible still if she has hurt herself and is waiting for help," said De Wet. He ran off down the path, shouting to the natives and waving his arms. The Gales saw them separate into three bands, and soon there were three groups of lights going away in different directions through the dark, and the shouting came back to them on the wind.

Mrs Gale thought, She could have taken the road back to the station, in which case she could be caught by car, even now.

She commanded her husband, "Take the car along the road and see."

"That's an idea," said the Major, and went off to the garage.

torch

---

*clamour,* a loud, continuous noise.

But that was the least ugly of the possibilities. What if she had been so blind with anger, *grief,* or whatever *emotion* it was that had driven her away, that she had simply run off into the veld not knowing where she went? She might at this moment be lying with a broken arm or leg. She might be pushing her way through grass higher than her head, falling over roots and rocks. She might be screaming for help somewhere for fear of wild animals, for if she crossed the valley into the hills there were leopards, lions, wild dogs. What if she had mistaken her direction and walked over the edge of the cliff in the dark? What if she had crossed the river and been taken by a crocodile? Anything might have happened. And then the fear of being alone on the veld, at night, knowing oneself lost. This was enough to send anyone off balance.

The silly little fool, the silly little fool. Anger and pity and *terror* confused in Mrs Gale until she was walking crazily up and down her garden. That night she hated her garden, that highly-cultivated piece of luxuriant growth, stuck in the middle of a country that could do this sort of thing to you suddenly. It was all the fault of the country! In a civilized sort of place, the girl would have caught a train to her mother, and a wire would have put everything right. Here, she might have killed herself.

Mrs Gale had no idea of how time was passing, until Major Gale returned and said that he had taken the ten miles to the station at seven miles an hour. At the

---

*grief,* deep sorrow.
*emotion,* any feeling that disturbs or excites the mind.
*terror,* very great fear.

station everyone was in bed, but the police were now waiting for news.

It was long after twelve. As for De Wet and his bands of searching natives, there was no sign of them. They would be miles away by this time.

Later she made some tea. They were so tired they could hardly move.

As the sun rose, De Wet returned over the veld. He said he had sent the natives home to sleep. They had found nothing. He also intended to sleep for an hour, and he would be back on the job by eight. Major Gale nodded, he recognized this as a necessary discipline. But after the man walked off across the veld towards his house, the two older people looked at each other and began to move after him. "He must not be alone," said Mrs Gale sensibly. "I shall make him some tea and see that he drinks it."

"He wants sleep," said Major Gale. His own eyes were red and heavy.

"I'll put something in his tea," said Mrs Gale. "He won't know it is there." Now she had something to do, she felt much better. Planning De Wet's comfort, she watched him turn in at his gate and disappear inside the house. They were some two hundred yards behind.

Suddenly there was a shout, and then a *commotion* of screams and shouting. The Gales ran fast along the remaining distance and burst into the front room, whitefaced and expecting the worst, in whatever form it might choose to present itself.

There was De Wet, his face ash grey with rage, bending over his wife, who was lying on the floor, shielding

---

*commotion,* a disturbance esp. among people.

her head with her arms, while he beat her shoulders with his closed *fists*.

Mrs Gale exclaimed, "Beating your wife!"

De Wet *flung* the girl away from him, and got to his feet. "She was there all the time," he said, half in temper, half in wonder. "She was hiding under the bed. She told me. When I came in she was sitting on the bed and laughing at me."

The girl beat her hands on the floor and said, laughing and crying at the same time, "Now you have to take some notice of me. Looking for me all night over the veld with your silly natives!"

"My God," said De Wet simply, giving up. He fell backwards into a chair and lay there, his eyes shut.

"So now you have to notice me," she shouted, but beginning though to look scared. "I have to pretend to run away, for you to sit up and take notice."

"Be quiet," said De Wet, breathing heavily. "Be quiet, if you don't want to get hurt really badly."

"Beating your wife," said Mrs Gale. "*Savages* behave better."

"Caroline, my dear," said Major Gale awkwardly. He moved towards the door.

"Take that woman out of here if you don't want me to beat her too," said De Wet to Major Gale.

Mrs Gale was by now crying with anger. "I'm not going," she said. "I'm not going. This poor child isn't safe with you."

"But what was it all about?" said Major Gale, laying

---

*fling,* to throw.
*savage,* a human being in an uncivilized state; also a fierce and cruel person.

44

fist

his hand kindly on the girl's shoulder. "What was it, my dear? What did you have to do it for, and make us all so worried?"

She began to cry. "Major Gale, I am sorry. I forgot myself. I got mad. I told him I was going to have a baby. I told him when I got back from your place. And all he said was That's fine. That's the first of them, he said. He didn't love me, or say he was pleased, or nothing."

"Dear Christ in hell," said De Wet wearily, "what do you make me do these things for? Do you think I want to beat you? Did you think I wasn't pleased. I keep telling you I want kids, I love kids."

"But you don't care about me," she said, crying bitterly.

"Don't I?" he said unhappily.

"Beating your wife when she's with child," said Mrs Gale. "You ought to be ashamed of yourself!" She advanced on the young man with her own fists *clenched*. "You ought to be beaten yourself, that's what you need."

Mrs De Wet lifted herself off the floor, rushed on Mrs Gale, pulled her back so that she nearly lost balance, and then flung herself on her husband. "Jack," she said, clinging to him, "I am so sorry, I am so sorry, Jack."

He put his arm round her. "There," he said simply with a tired voice, "don't cry. We got mixed up, that's all."

Major Gale said to his wife in a low voice, "Come Caroline. Come. Leave them to sort it out."

"And what if he loses his temper again and decides

*clench,* to close tightly.

to kill her this time?" demanded Mrs Gale.

De Wet got to his feet, lifting his wife with him. "Go away now, Mrs Major," he said. "Get out of here. You've done enough damage."

"I've done enough damage?" she shouted. "And what have I done?"

"Oh nothing at all," he said, bitterly. "Nothing at all. But please go and leave my wife in the future, Mrs Major."

"Come, Caroline, p l e a s e," said Major Gale.

She allowed herself to be drawn out of the room. Her head was aching so that the bright morning light entered her eyes in a wave of pain.

"Mrs Major," she said, "Mrs Major!"

"He was upset," said her husband.

"So it was all my fault," she said, after a silence.

"He didn't say so."

"I thought that was what he was saying. He beats his wife and says it is my fault."

"It was no one's fault," said Major Gale.

They reached the gate, and entered the garden, which was now musical with birds.

"A lovely morning," remarked Major Gale.

"Next time you get an assistant," she said finally, "get people of our kind. These might be savages, the way they behave."

And that was the last word she would ever say on the subject.

# Questions

1. What is the country like?

2. In what way does it influence Major and Mrs Gale?

3. What kind of people are they?

4. How are relations between them?

5. How has Mrs Gale fought her loneliness?

6. Why does she dislike the idea of another woman on the farm?

7. What kind of people are the De Wets?

8. In what way is Mrs De Wet different from the picture Mrs Gale has formed of the assistant's wife?

9. How is the assistant?

10. What does he have in common with Major Gale?

11. How does the young woman experience her loneliness?

12. Why does Mrs De Wet's situation upset Mrs Gale?

13. What does Mrs De Wet do to attract her husband's attention to her problem?

14. Why does Mrs Gale fail to understand the young woman?

# The Black Madonna

Zambesia is a tough sunburnt country with no tendency towards the arts. Why this should be so is hard to say. There have been states with the same conditions that have produced art, though perhaps with the left hand. The Zambesians, however, show an almost *wistful* respect when an artist does appear among them.

Consider, for instance, the case of Michele.

He came out of the *internment camp* at the time when Italy was made an *ally,* during the Second World War. It was a difficult time for the *authorities,* because it is one thing to be responsible for thousands of prisoners of war whom one must treat according to certain recognized standards. It is another to be faced, and from one day to the next, with these same thousands changed into allies. Some of the thousands stayed where they were in the camps, they were fed and housed there at least. Others became farm *labourers,* though not many. The farmers did not know how to handle farm labourers who were also white men – such a thing had never happened in Zambesia before. Some did occasional jobs around the towns, keeping a sharp eye out for trade unions, who would neither admit them as members nor agree to their working.

---

*wistful,* rather sad, as if longing for something.
*internment camp,* camp where prisoners from the enemy side are kept while a war is going on.
*ally,* one of two or more persons or nations joined together against a common enemy.
*authorities,* government officials.
*labourer,* unskilled worker.

It was a difficult period for these men, but fortunately not long, as the war soon ended and they were able to go home.

It was difficult, too, for the authorities, as has been pointed out. For that reason they were most willing to take what advantages they could of the situation. There could be no doubt of the fact that Michele was such an advantage.

His *talents* were first discovered when he was still a prisoner of war. A church was built in the camp, and Michele painted its walls. It became a show-place, that little church in the prisoners' camp, with its white walls covered all over with *frescoes* showing *peasants* gathering *grapes,* beautiful Italian girls dancing, and dark-eyed children. In the middle of crowded scenes of Italian life appeared a smiling Virgin Mary and her child.

*Culture*-loving ladies with permission to be taken inside the camp would say, "Poor thing, how *homesick* he must be." And they would beg to be allowed to leave half a crown for the artist. Some were angry and upset. He was a prisoner of war, after all, and what right had he to protest? They felt these paintings as a sort of protest. What was there in Italy that we did not have right here in Westonville, the capital of Zambesia? Were there not sunshine and mountains and fat babies and pretty girls here? Did we not grow – if not grapes, at least oranges and flowers in plenty?

---

*talent,* a special ability or skill.
*fresco,* a picture painted directly on the wall.
*peasant,* one who works and lives on the land.
*culture,* here, educated tastes in art, music and literature.
*homesick,* longing for home.

grapes

But when Michele was free, his talent was remembered. He was spoken of as 'that Italian artist'. As a matter of fact, he was a bricklayer, and it is possible that his frescoes would not have been noticed at all in a country where picture-covered walls were more common.

When one of the visiting ladies came rushing out to the camp in her own car, to ask him to paint her children, he said he was not fit for the job. But at last he agreed. He took a room in the town and did some nice pictures of the children. Then he painted the children of a great number of the first lady's friends. He charged ten shillings a time.

Then he went off to his room with a friend and stayed there drinking red wine from the Cape and talking about home. While the money lasted he could not be persuaded to do any more paintings.

He was felt to lack respect for work and *gratitude*. One of the ladies tracked him down, found him lying on a camp-bed under a tree with a bottle of wine, and spoke to him severely about the *barbarity* of Mussolini and the weakness and lack of spirit of the Italian people. Then she demanded that he should instantly paint a picture of herself in her new evening dress. He refused, and she went home very angry.

It happened that she was the wife of one of our most important citizens, a General or something of that kind, who was at that time planning a *military tattoo* for the *civilian* population. The whole of Westonville had

---

*gratitude,* desire to pay back kindness shown.
*barbarity,* cruel behaviour.
*military tattoo,* an outdoor show at night given by soldiers.
*civilian,* one who is not in the armed forces.

been discussing this show for weeks. We were all bored to death by dances, balls, *fairs* and other *charitable* entertainment. It is not too much to say that while some were dying for freedom, others were dancing for it. There comes a limit to everything. Though, of course, when the end of the war actually came and the thousands of *troops* stationed in the country had to go home – in short, when enjoying themselves would no longer be a duty, many were heard to exclaim that life would never be the same again.

In the meantime, the Tattoo would make a nice change for us all. The military gentlemen responsible for the idea did not think of it in these terms. They thought of improving *morale* by giving us some idea of what war was really like. Headlines in the newspapers were not enough. And in order to bring it all home to us, they planned to destroy a village by *shell*-fire before our very eyes.

First, the village had to be built.

It appears that the General and his men stood around in the red dust of the *parade-ground* under a burning sun for the whole of one day, surrounded by building materials, while a large crowd of African labourers ran around with boards and nails, trying to make something that looked like a village. It became clear that they would have to build a proper village in order to destroy it, and this would cost more than was

---

*fair,* a sale of goods to collect money for those in need.
*charitable,* giving money to those in need.
*troops,* soldiers.
*morale,* spirit and confidence.
*shell,* here a bomb.
*parade-ground,* place where the troops exercise.

allowed for the whole show. The General went home in a bad temper, and his wife said what they needed was an artist, they needed Michele. This was not because she wanted to do Michele a good turn. She could not stand the thought of him lying around singing while there was work to be done. She refused to see him herself when her husband said he would be damned if he would ask favours of any little *wop*. She solved the problem for him in her own way: a certain Captain Stocker was sent out to fetch him.

The Captain found him on the same camp-bed under the same tree, in rolled-up trousers, and an open shirt, unshaven, mildly drunk, with a bottle of wine standing beside him on the ground. He was singing a song so wild and so sad that the Captain was uncomfortable. A year ago, this man had been an enemy to be shot on sight. Six months ago, he had been an enemy prisoner. Now he lay with his knees up, in an untidy shirt that had certainly once been military. The Captain felt a strong desire for Michele to *salute* him.

"Piselli!" he said sharply.

Michele turned his head and looked at the Captain. "Good morning," he said kindly.

"You are wanted," said the Captain.

"Who?" said Michele. He sat up, a rather fat, dark little man. His eyes were resentful.

"The authorities."

"The war is over?"

The Captain was a large man, blond, and wherever

---

*wop,* a very bad (slang) name for an Italian.
*salute,* in the armed forces, to raise the hand to the forehead to show respect.

his flesh showed, it was brick-red. His eyes were small and blue and angry. "No, it is not over," he said. "Your help is needed."

"For the war?"

"For the war effort. I take it you are interested in defeating the Germans?"

Michele looked at the Captain. The little dark-eyed *artisan* looked at the great blond officer with his cold blue eyes and his narrow mouth. He looked and said, "I am very interested in the end of the war."

"Well?" said the Captain between his teeth.

"The pay?" said Michele.

"You will be paid."

Michele stood up. He lifted the bottle against the sun, cleaned his mouth out with a little wine and poured what was left on to the red earth.

"I am ready," he said. He went with the Captain to the waiting *lorry* where he climbed in beside the driver's seat and not, as the Captain had expected, into the back of the lorry. When they arrived at the parade-ground the officers had left a message that the Captain would be personally responsible for Michele and for the village, as well as for the hundred or so labourers who were sitting around waiting for orders.

The Captain explained what was wanted. Michele nodded. Then he waved his hands at the Africans. "I do not need these people," he said.

"You will do it yourself – a village?"

"Yes."

"With no help?"

---

*artisan,* skilled workman; artist.
*lorry,* truck.

Michele smiled for the first time. "I will do it."

The Captain hesitated. He did not approve of white men doing heavy *manual* work. He said, "I will keep six to do the heavy work." Then he went over and told all but six of the Africans to go home. He came back with them to Michele.

"It is hot," said Michele.

"Very," said the Captain. They were standing in the middle of the parade-ground. Along its edge there were trees, grass, shade. Here nothing but red dust.

"I am thirsty," said Michele. He grinned. The Captain felt his stiff lips loosen unwillingly in reply. The two pairs of eyes met. It was a moment of understanding. For the Captain the little Italian had suddenly become human. "I will arrange it," he said, and went

*manual,* done by hand.

off. By the time he had explained the position to the right people, filled in papers and made arrangements, it was late afternoon. He returned to the parade ground with a case of Cape *brandy,* to find Michele and the six black men seated together under a tree. Michele was singing an Italian song to them and they were singing with him. The sight made the Captain feel sick. He came up, and the Africans stood to attention. Michele continued to sit.

"You said you would do the work yourself?"

"Yes, I did."

The Captain then sent the Africans home. They left with friendly looks towards Michele, who waved at them. The Captain was red with anger. "You have not started yet?"

"How long have I?"

"Three weeks."

"Then there is plenty of time," said Michele looking at the bottle of brandy in the Captain's hand. In the other were two glasses. "It is evening," he pointed out. The Captain hesitated for a moment. Then he sat down on the grass, and poured out two brandies.

"Cheers," said Michele.

"Cheers," said the Captain. Three weeks, he was thinking. Three weeks with this damned little *Itie*! He emptied his glass and filled it again, and placed it in the grass. The grass was cool and soft.

"It is nice here," said Michele. "We will have a good time together. Even in a war, there are times of happiness and friendship. I drink to the end of the war."

---

*brandy,* a spirit made from wine.
*Itie,* Italian (slang).

Next day, the Captain did not arrive at the parade-ground until after lunch. He found Michele under the trees with a bottle. Sheets of ceiling board had been put up at one end of the parade-ground in such a way that they formed two walls and part of a third and a piece of steep roof supported on *struts*.

"What's that?" said the Captain, furious.

"The church," said Michele.

"Wha-at?"

"You will see. Later. It is very hot." He looked at the brandy bottle that lay on its side on the ground. The Captain went to the lorry and returned with the case of brandy. They drank. Time passed. It was a long time since the Captain had sat on grass under a tree. It was a long time, for that matter, since he had drunk so much. He always drank a great deal, but only at certain times and seasons. He was a disciplined man. Here, sitting on the grass beside this little man whom he still could not help thinking of as an enemy, it was not that he let his self-discipline go, but that he felt himself to be something different. He was, for the time being, set outside his normal behaviour. Michele did not count. He listened to Michele talking about Italy, and it seemed to him he was listening to a savage speaking, as if he heard tales from the South Sea islands where a man like himself might very well go just once in his life. He found himself saying he would like to make a trip to Italy after the war. Actually, he was attracted only by the North and the Northern people. He had visited Germany, under Hitler, and though it was not the time

*strut,* a bar which supports something.

to say so, had found it very satisfactory. Then Michele sang him some Italian songs. He sang Michele some English songs. Then Michele took out photographs of his wife and children, who lived in a village in the mountains of North Italy. He asked the Captain if he was married. The Captain never spoke of his private affairs.

He had spent all his life in one or other of the African

colonies as a policeman or *magistrate* or in other posts in the department of public service. When the war started military life came easily to him. But he hated city life, and had his own reasons for wishing the war over. Mostly, he had been in *bush*-stations with one or two other white men, or by himself, far from civilization. He had relations with native women, and from time to time visited the city where his wife lived with her parents and the children. He was always deeply afraid she was unfaithful to him. Recently he had even appointed a private detective to watch her. Army friends coming from L . . . where his wife was, spoke of her at parties, enjoying herself. When the war ended, she would not find it so easy to have a good time. And why did he not simply live with her and be done with it? The fact was, he could not. He could not bear to think of his wife for too long. She was that part of his life he had never been able to bring under control.

Yet he spoke of her now to Michele, and of his favourite bush-wife, Nadya. He told Michele the story of his life until the shadows grew long. He got unsteadily to his feet and said "There is work to be done. You are being paid to work."

"I will show you my church when the light goes."

The sun went down, darkness fell, and Michele made the Captain drive his lorry to the parade-ground a couple of hundred yards away and switch on his lights. Instantly, a white church sprang up from the shapes and shadows of the bits of board.

---

*magistrate,* civil officer like a police judge or Justice of the Peace.
*bush,* here, wild land, covered with trees and bushes, esp. in Africa.

"Tomorrow, some houses," said Michele *cheerfully*.

At the end of the week, the space at the end of the parade-ground had crazy *constructions* of board over it that looked in the sunlight like nothing on this earth. Privately, it upset the Captain. It was like a bad dream that these strange shapes should be able to persuade him, with the effects of light and dark, that they were a village. At night, the Captain drove up his lorry, switched on the lights, and there it was, the village, solid and real. Then, in the morning sunlight, there was nothing there, just bits of board stuck in the sand.

"It is finished," said Michele.

"You were engaged for three weeks," said the Captain. He did not want it to end, this holiday from himself.

Michele *shrugged*. "The army is rich," he said. Now to avoid curious eyes, they sat inside the shade of the church, with the case of brandy between them. The Captain talked, about his wife, about women. He could not stop talking.

Michele listened. Once he said, "When I go home – when I go home – I shall open my arms . . ." He opened them, wide. He closed his eyes. Tears ran down his cheeks. "I shall take my wife in my arms, and I shall ask nothing, nothing. I do not care. It is enough, it is enough. I shall ask no questions and I shall be happy."

The Captain stared before him, suffering. He thought how he feared his wife. She was gay and hard.

---

*cheerful,* happy, gay.
*construction,* that which is built.
*shrug,* to show doubt, lack of interest etc. by drawing up the shoulders.

She laughed at him. She had been laughing at him ever since they married. Since the war, she had taken to calling him names like Little Hitler. "Go ahead, my Little Hitler," she had cried last time they met. "Go ahead. If you want to waste your money on private detectives, go ahead. But don't think I don't know what you do when you're in the bush. I don't care what you do, but remember that I know it . . ."

The Captain remembered her saying it. And there sat Michele, saying, "It's a pleasure for the rich, my friend, detectives and the law. Ah, my friend, to be together with my wife again, and the children, that is all I ask of life. That and wine and food and singing in the evening." And tears wetted his cheeks and dropped on to his shirt.

That a man should cry, good Lord! thought the Captain. And without shame! He seized the bottle and drank.

Three days before the great occasion, some officers of high rank came walking through the dust, and found Michele and the Captain sitting together, singing. The Captain's shirt was open down the front.

The Captain stood to attention with the bottle in his hand, and Michele stood to attention too, out of sympathy with his friend. The officers drew the Captain aside – they were all friends of his – and said, what the hell did he think he was doing? And why wasn't the village finished?

Then they went away.

"Tell them it is finished," said Michele. "Tell them I want to go."

"No," said the Captain, "no. Michele, what would you do if your wife . . ."

"This world is a good place. We should be happy – that is all."

"Michele . . ."

"I want to go. There is nothing to do. They paid me yesterday."

"Sit down, Michele. Three more days and then it's finished."

"Then I shall paint the inside of the church as I painted the one in the camp."

The Captain laid himself down on some boards and went to sleep. When he woke, Michele was surrounded by the pots of paint he had used on the outside of the village. Just in front of the Captain was a picture of a black girl. She was young and *plump*. She wore a blue dress and her shoulders came soft and bare out of it. On her back was a baby. Her face was turned towards the Captain and she was smiling.

"That's Nadya," said the Captain. "Nadya . . ." He *moaned* loudly. He looked at the black girl and shut his eyes. He opened them, and mother and child were still there. Michele was very carefully drawing thin yellow circles around the heads of the black girl and her child.

"Good God," said the Captain, "you can't do that."

"Why not?"

"You can't have a black Madonna."

"She was a peasant. This is a peasant. Black peasant Madonna for black country."

"This is a German village," said the Captain.

"This is my Madonna," said Michele angrily. "Your German village and my Madonna. I paint this picture

---

*plump,* well-filled or rounded out.
*moan,* to make a low sound of grief and pain.

as an *offering* to the Madonna. She is pleased – I feel it."

The Captain lay down again. He was feeling ill. He went back to sleep. When he woke for the second time, it was dark. Michele had brought in a lamp, and by its

---

*offering,* gift.

light was working on the long wall. A bottle of brandy stood beside him. He painted until long after midnight, and the Captain lay on his side and watched, as a man suffering in a dream. Then they both went to sleep on the boards. The whole of the next day Michele stood painting black Madonnas, black *saints,* black angels.

Outside, troops were practising in the sunlight, bands were playing and motor-cycles roared up and down. But Michele painted on. The Captain lay on his back, drinking and *muttering* about his wife. Then he would say, "Nadya, Nadya," and burst into tears.

Towards nightfall the troops went away. The officers came back, and the Captain went off with them to show how the village sprang into being when the great lights at the end of the parade-ground were switched on. They all looked at the village in silence. They switched the lights off, and there were only tall boards leaning like gravestones in the moonlight. On went the lights – and there was the village. They were silent, as filled with suspicion. Like the Captain, they seemed to feel it was not right. It was unfair, it was a trick. And very disturbing.

"Clever chap, that Italian of yours," said the General.

The Captain who had been extremely correct until this moment, suddenly came rocking up to the General, and steadied himself by laying his hands on the General's shoulder. *"Bloody* Wops," he said. "Tell

---

*saint,* a holy person.
*mutter,* to speak words in a low voice with lips almost closed.
*bloody,* damned.

you what, though, there's one Itie that's some good. Yes, there is. I'm telling you. He's a friend of mine, actually."

The General looked at him. Then he nodded at his men. The Captain was taken away *for disciplinary purposes*. It was decided, however, that he must be ill, nothing else could account for such a behaviour. He was put to bed in his own room with a nurse to watch him.

He woke twenty-four hours later, *sober* for the first time in weeks. He slowly remembered what had happened. Then he sprang out of bed and rushed into his clothes. The nurse was just in time to see him run down the path and leap into his lorry.

*for disciplinary purposes,* to be punished.
*sober,* not drunk.

He drove at top speed to the parade-ground, which was flooded with light in such a way that the village did not seem to exist. Everything was in full swing. The cars were three deep around the square. The place was packed with people. On the square, troops were getting ready, machine-guns were being dragged up and down, bands played, motor-cycles roared.

As the Captain parked the lorry, all this activity came to an end, and the lights went out. The Captain began running around the outside of the square to reach the place where the guns were hidden in a mess of net and branches. He was *gasping* with the effort. He was a big man, and not used to exercise, and filled with brandy. He had only one idea in his mind – to stop the

*gasp,* to be out of breath.

guns firing, to stop them at all costs.

Luckily, there seemed to be a delay. The lights were still out. Then the lights switched on for a short moment, and the village sprang into existence just for long enough to show large red crosses all over a white building beside the church. Then moonlight flooded everything again, and the crosses disappeared. "Oh, the bloody fool!" gasped the Captain, running, running, as if for his life. He was no longer trying to reach the guns. He was cutting across a corner of the square direct to the church. He could hear some officers cursing behind him, "Who put those red crosses there? Who? We can't fire on the Red Cross."

The Captain reached the church as the searchlights burst on. Inside, Michele was kneeling on the earth looking at his first Madonna. "They are going to kill my Madonna," he said unhappily.

"Come away, Michele, come away."

"They are going to . . ."

The Captain grabbed his arm and pulled. There was dead silence outside. Then a voice came through the loudspeakers. "The village that is about to be *shelled* is an English village, not as represented on the programme, a German village. Repeat, the village that is about to be shelled is . . ."

"Michele," cried the Captain, "g e t o u t o f h e r e."

There was a roar. The church seemed to melt around them into flame. Then they were running away from it, the Captain holding Michele tight by the arm. "Get down," he shouted suddenly, and threw Michele to the earth. He flung himself down beside him. Looking

*shell,* to bomb.

from under his arm, he heard the explosion, saw a great pillar of smoke and flame, and the village fell into pieces. Michele was on his knees staring at his Madonna in the light from the flames. He looked horrible, quite white, and blood ran from his hair down one cheek.

"They shelled my Madonna," he said.

"Oh, damn it, you can paint another one," said the Captain. His own voice seemed strange to him, like a dream voice. He was certainly crazy, as mad as Michele himself . . . He got up, pulled Michele to his feet, and marched him towards the edge of the field. There he was met by the ambulance people. Michele was taken off to hospital, and the Captain was sent back to bed.

A week passed. The Captain was in a darkened room. That he was having some kind of *breakdown* was clear, and two nurses stood guard over him. Sometimes he lay quiet, sometimes he muttered to himself. Sometimes he sang in a thick voice bits out of opera, of Italian songs, and – over and over again – There's a Long Long Trail. He was not thinking of anything at all. He turned away from all thoughts of Michele as if they were dangerous. When, therefore, a cheerful female voice told him that a friend had come to cheer him up, and it would do him good to have some company, and he saw a white *bandage* moving towards him in the dark, he turned sharp over on to his side, face to the wall.

"Go away," he said. "Go away, Michele."

"I have come to see you," said Michele. "I have brought you a present."

The Captain slowly turned over. There was Michele, standing cheerful in the dark room. "You fool," he said. "You messed everything up. What did you paint those crosses for?"

"It was a hospital," said Michele. "In a village there is a hospital, and on the hospital the Red Cross, the beautiful Red Cross – no?"

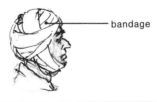 bandage

---

*breakdown,* a failure of health.

"I was nearly *court-martialled*."

"It was my fault," said Michele. "I was drunk."

"I was responsible."

"How could you be responsible when I did it? But it is all over. Are you better?"

"Well, I suppose those crosses saved your life."

"I did not think," said Michele. "I was remembering the kindness of the Red Cross people when we were prisoners."

"Oh shut up, shut up, shut up."

"I have brought you a present."

The Captain looked through the dark. Michele was holding up a picture. It was of a smiling native woman with a baby on her back.

Michele said, "You did not like the *haloes*. So this time no haloes. For the Captain – no Madonna." He laughed. "You like it? It is for you. I painted it for you."

"God damn you!" said the Captain.

"You do not like it?" said Michele, very hurt.

The Captain closed his eyes. "What are you going to do next?" he asked tiredly.

Michele laughed again. "Mrs Pannerhurst, the lady of the General, she wants me to paint her picture in her white dress. So I paint it."

"You should be proud to."

"Silly *bitch*. She thinks I am good. They know nothing – savages. Not you, Captain, you are my friend. But these people, they know nothing."

---

*court-martialled,* put before a military court for breaking the army laws.

*halo,* a ring of light around a holy person's head.

*bitch,* a female dog; here, an unpleasant, ill-tempered woman.

The Captain lay quiet. Fury was gathering in him.

"These people," said Michele. "They do not know a good picture from a bad picture. I paint, I paint, this way, that way. There is the picture – I look at it and laugh inside myself." Michele laughed out loud. "They say, he is a Michelangelo, this one, and try to pay me less. Michele – Michelangelo – that is a joke, no?"

The Captain said nothing.

"But for you I painted this picture to remind you of our good times with the village. You are my friend. I will always remember you."

The Captain stared at the black girl. Her smile at him was half *innocence,* half *malice.*

"Get out," he said suddenly.

Michele came closer and bent over to see the Captain's face. "You wish me to go?" He sounded unhappy. "You saved my life. I was a fool that night. But I was thinking of my offering to the Madonna – I was a fool, I say it myself. I was drunk. We are fools when we are drunk."

"Get out of here," said the Captain again.

For a moment the white bandage did not move. Then it swept downwards in a bow.

Michele turned towards the door.

"And take that bloody picture with you."

Silence. Then the Captain saw Michele reach out for the picture. He straightened himself and stood to attention, holding the picture with one hand, and keeping the other stiffly by his side. Then he saluted the Captain.

---

*innocence,* lack of moral wrong.
*malice,* ill will.

"Yes, s i r," he said, and he turned and went out of the door with the picture.

The Captain lay still. He felt – what did he feel? He felt pain. It hurt to breathe. He realized he was unhappy. Yes, a terrible unhappiness was filling him, slowly, slowly. He was unhappy because Michele had gone. Nothing ever hurt the Captain in all his life as much as that *mocking* Yes, sir. Nothing. He

---

*mock,* to laugh at, to make fun of.

turned his face to the wall and wept. But silently. Not a sound escaped him, for the fear the nurses might hear.

## Questions

1. When does the story take place?

2. How do the historical events influence the life of people in Zambesia?

3. What prejudices influence their lives?

4. Why does Michele's behaviour upset the ladies of Westonville?

5. How do his artistic qualities prove to be of advantage to the authorities?

6. How does friendship develop between the Captain and Michele?

7. What is the difference between the two men's relations to their families?

8. How does their friendship change the Captain's life?

9. How does the Captain save his friend?

10. Why does he refuse to accept Michele's gift and break off their friendship?

# The Words He Said

lemon

On the morning of the *braavleis,* Dad kept saying to Moira, as if he thought it was a joke, "Moy, it's going to rain." First she did not hear him, then she turned her head, slow and calm, and looked at him so that he remembered what she said the day before. He became red in the face and went indoors out of her way. The day before, he said to her but speaking to me, "What's got into Moys head? Is the braavleis for her *engagement* or what?"

It was because Moira spent all morning cooking her *lemon* cake for the braavleis, and she went over to Sam the butcher's to order the best meat.

---

*braavleis,* outdoor feast with *grilled* food, that is, cooked over a fire.
*engagement,* a promise of marriage.

All the cold season she was not cooking, she was not helping Mom in the house at all, she was not taking an interest in life, and Dad was saying to Mom, "Oh get the girl to town or something, don't let her wander about here, who does she think she is?"

Mom just said, quiet and calm, the way she was with Dad when they did not agree, "Oh let her alone, Dickson." When Mom and Dad were agreeing, they called each other Mom and Dad. When they were against each other, it was Marion and Dickson, and that is how it was for the whole of the dry season. Moira was pale and absent-minded and would not talk to me, and it was no fun for me, I can tell you.

"What's this for?" Dad said once about half-way through the season, when Moira stayed in bed three days and Mom let her. "Has he said anything to her or hasn't he?"

Mom just said, "She's sick, Dickson."

But I could see what he said had gone into her, because I was in our bedroom when Mom came to Moira.

Mom sat down on the bed, but at the bottom of it, and she was worried. "Listen girl," said Mom. "I don't want to interfere, I don't want to do that, but what did Greg say?"

Moira was not properly in bed. She just lay there, not reading anything, looking out of the window over at the big *water-tanks* across the railway lines. Her face looked bad, and she said, "Oh, leave me alone, Mom."

Mom said, "Sometimes boys say a thing, and they don't mean it the way we think. They feel they have to

---

*water-tank,* a large container for water.

say it. It's not that they don't mean it, but they mean it different."

"He didn't say anything at all," said Moira. "Why should he?"

"Why don't you go into town and stay with Aunt Nora a while? You can come back for the holidays when Greg comes back."

"Oh let me alone," said Moira, and she began to cry. That was the first time she cried. At least, in front of Mom. I used to hear her cry at night when she thought I was asleep.

"He didn't say anything, Mom," I said. "But I know what happened."

Moira looked up and said, "Get that kid away from me."

They could not get me away from Moira, because there were only two bedrooms, and I always slept with Moira. But she would not speak to me that night at all.

It was at last year's braavleis that it happened. Moira was not keen on Greg then, I know for a fact, because she was sweet on Jordan. Greg was mostly at the Cape at college, but he came back for the first time in a year, and I saw him looking at Moira. She was pretty then, because she had finished her *matric* and spent all her time making herself pretty. She was eighteen, and her hair was *wavy*, because the rains had started. Greg was on the other side of the *bonfire*, and he came walking around it up to Moira. Moira smiled politely, she wanted Jordan to sit by her, and she was

---

*matric,* short for *matriculation,* a final school examination.
*wavy,* having waves.
*bonfire,* see illustration p. 78.

bonfire

afraid he wouldn't if he saw her occupied by Greg.

"Moira Hughes?" he said. Moira smiled, and he said, "I wouldn't have known you."

"Go on," I said, "you've known us always."

They did not hear me. They were just looking. It was peculiar.

Because of the way she was looking at him, I looked

at him too, but I did not think he was *handsome*. The holidays before, when I was sweet on Greg Jackson, I naturally thought he was handsome, but now he was just ordinary. His hair was red, and his *freckles* were thick, because naturally the sun is no good for people with white skin and freckles.

But he wasn't bad, particularly when he was in his reasonable mood. Then he was quiet and grown-up, and some of the *gang* didn't like it, because he was better than us. He was the only one of the gang to go to university at the Cape.

After they had finished looking at each other, he just sat down in the grass in the place Moira was keeping for Jordan, and Moira did not once look around for Jordan. They did not say anything else, just went on sitting, and when the big dance began with people holding hands around the bonfire, they stood at one side watching.

That was all that happened at the braavleis, and that was all the words he said. Next day, Greg went on a shooting trip with his father who was the man at the garage, and they went right up the Zambesi valley, and Greg did not come back to our station.

I knew Moira was hoping for a letter, because she always went herself to the post office on mail days. But there was no letter. But after that she said to Jordan, "No thanks, I don't feel like it," when he asked her to go into town.

She did not take any notice af any of the gang after

---

*handsome,* good-looking.
*freckles,* brown spots on the skin.
*gang,* any group of people who meet regularly.

that, though before she had been the leader of the gang, even over the boys.

That was when she stopped being pretty again. She looked as she did before she left school and was working hard for her matric. She was too thin, and the curl went out of her hair, and she didn't bother to curl it either.

All that dry season she did nothing, and hardly spoke, and did not sing. I knew it was because of that minute when Greg and she looked at each other. That was all. And when I thought of it, I could feel hot and cold down my back.

Well, on the day before the braavleis, like I said, Moira was on the veranda, and she had on her the dress she wore last year to the braavleis. Greg had come back for the holidays the night before. We knew he had, because his mother said so when Mom met her at the store. But he did not come to our house. I did not like to see Moira's face, but I had to keep on looking at it, it was so sad, and her eyes were sore. Mom kissed her, putting both her arms around her, but Moira pushed her away.

Mom sighed, and then I saw Dad looking at her, and the look they gave each other was most peculiar, it made me feel very peculiar again. And then Moira started in on her lemon cake, and went to the butcher's and that was when Dad said that about the braavleis being for the engagement. Moira looked at him, with her eyes all black and sad and said, "Why have you got it in for me Dad, what have I done?"

Dad said, "Greg's not going to marry you. Now he's got to college, and going to be a doctor, he won't be after you."

Moira was smiling, her lips small and angry.

Mom said, "Why Dickson, Moira's got her matric and she's educated, what't got into your head?"

Dad said, "I'm telling you, that's all."

Moira said, very grown-up and quiet, "Why are you trying to spoil it for me, Dad? I haven't said anything about marrying, have I? And what have I done to you, anyway?"

Dad didn't like that. He went red, and he laughed, but he didn't like it. And he was quiet for a bit at least.

After lunch, when she'd finished with the cake she was sitting on the veranda when Jordan went past across to the store, and she called out, "Hi, Jordan, come and talk to me."

Now I know for a fact that Jordan wasn't sweet on Moira any more, he was sweet on Beth from the store, because I know for a fact he kissed her at the last station dance, I saw him. He shouted out, "Thanks Moy, but I'm on my way."

"Oh, please yourself then," said Moira, friendly and nice, but I knew she was angry.

Anyway, he came in, and I've never seen Moira so nice to anyone, not even when she was sweet on him, and certainly never to Greg. She took Jordan into the kitchen to see the lemon cake, and she said, slow and surprised, "But we haven't got enough bread for the sandwiches, Mom what are you thinking of?"

Mom said, quick and angry, because she was proud of her kitchen, "What do you mean? No one's going to eat sandwiches with all the meat you've ordered."

"I think we need more bread," said Moira. And she said to me in the same voice, slow and lazy, "Just run over to the Jackson's and see if they can let us have some bread."

At this I didn't say anything, and Mom did not say anything either, and it was lucky Dad didn't hear. I looked at Mom, and she made no sign, so I went across the railway lines to the garage, and at the back of the garage was the Jackson's house, and there was Greg Jackson reading a book about the body because he was going to be a doctor.

"Mom says, can you let us have some bread?" I said.

He put down the book, and said, "Oh, hullo, Betty."

"Hullo," I said.

"But the store is open."

"We want some *stale* bread," I said, "Moy's making some *stuffing* for the chicken, our bread's all fresh."

"Mom's at the store," he said, "but help yourself."

So I went into the kitchen and got the bread, and came out and said "Thanks" and walked past him.

He said, "Don't mention it." Then, when I was nearly gone, he said, "And how's Moy?" And I said, "Fine, but I haven't seen much of her these holidays because she's busy with Jordan." I went away, and sure enough there he was coming up behind me, and then he was beside me.

"I'll drop over and say hullo," said Greg, and I felt peculiar I can tell you, because what I was thinking was, Well! If this is love.

When we got near our house, Moira and Jordan were side by side on the veranda wall, and Moy was

---

*stale,* (of food) no longer fresh.
*stuffing,* preparation made mainly of bread, packed inside a chicken or other meat and cooked with it.

laughing and I knew she had seen Greg coming because of the way she laughed.

Dad was not on the veranda, so I could see Mom had got him to stay indoors.

"I've brought you the bread, Moy," I said, and with this I went into the kitchen. There was Mom, and she was looking more peculiar than I've ever seen her. I was sure she wanted to laugh, but she was sighing all the time. Because of the sighing I knew she had quarreled with Dad.

There sat Mom and I in the kitchen, smiling at each other off and on in a peculiar way. When we looked out on the veranda about half an hour later Jordan was gone, and Greg and Moira were sitting on the veranda wall. And I can tell you she looked so pretty again. It was strange her getting pretty like that so sudden.

That was about five, and Greg went back to supper at home, and Moira did not eat anything, she was in our room curling her hair, because she and Greg were going for a walk.

"Don't go too far, it's going to rain," Mom said, but Moira said, sweet and nice, "Don't worry, Mom, I can look after myself."

Mom and Dad said nothing to each other all the evening.

I went to bed early for a change, so I'd be there when Moy got in, although I was thirteen that season and now my bedtime was up to ten o'clock.

Mom and Dad went to bed, although I could see Mom was worried, because there was a storm blowing up, the dry season was due to end.

I lay awake saying to myself, Sleep, sleep go away, come again another day, but I went to sleep, and when

I woke up, the room was full of the smell of rain, of the earth wet with rain, the light was on and Moira was in the room.

"Have the rains come?" I said, and then I woke right up and saw of course they hadn't, because the air was dry as sand, and Moira said, "Oh shut up and go to sleep."

She did not look pretty as much as being different from how I'd seen her, her face was soft and smiling, and her eyes were different. She had blue eyes most of the time, but now they seemed quite black and her hair was all curled and brushed.

She sat smiling on the edge of her bed, and when I said, "What did he say, Moy?" she just turned her head and made her eyes thin and black at me, and I saw I'd better go to sleep. But I knew something she didn't know I knew, because she had some dead *jacaranda* flowers in her hair, so that meant she and Greg were at the water-tanks. There were only two jacaranda trees at our station, and they were at the big water-tanks for the engines, so if they were at the water-tanks, they must have been kissing, because it was *romantic* at the tanks. It was the end of October, and the jacaranda flowers were dropping, and the tanks looked as if they were standing in pools of blue water.

Well, next morning Moy was already up when I woke. She was singing, and she began ironing her *muslin* dress that she made for last Christmas, even before breakfast.

---

*jacaranda,* tree with pale-purple flowers found in hot countries.
*romantic,* beautiful, lovely.
*muslin,* a kind of fine, soft cotton cloth.

After breakfast, we sat around, because it was Sunday, and Dad didn't have to be at the station office because there weren't any trains on Sundays. And Dad kept grinning at Moira and saying, "I think it's going to rain," and she pretended she didn't know what he meant, until at last she jumped when he said it and turned herself and looked at him just the way she did the day before. That was when he went red in the face, and said, "Can't you take a joke these days?" Moira looked away from him with her *eyebrows* up, Mom

eyebrow

sighed, and then he said very angrily, "I'll leave you all to it, just tell me when you're in a better temper," and with this he took the newspaper inside to the bedroom.

Anybody could see it wasn't going to rain properly that day, the clouds were great big white ones, all silver and hardly any black in them.

Moy didn't eat any dinner, but went on sitting on the veranda, wearing her dress that was muslin, white with red spots. After dinner, time was very slow, and it was a long time before Greg came down off the Jackson's veranda, and came walking slowly along the avenue. I was watching Moy's face, and she couldn't keep the smile off it. She got paler and paler until he got beneath our veranda. She looked at him in such a way that I got goose-flesh all over.

Then he jumped up our steps on to the veranda, and said, "Hoy, Moy, how's it?" I thought she was going to fall right off the veranda wall, and her face had gone all different again.

"How are you, Gregory?" said Moira, all calm and proud.

"Oh, getting along," he said, and I could see he felt awkward, because he didn't look at her once, and his skin was all red around the freckles. She didn't say anything, and she was looking at him as if she couldn't believe it was him.

"I hope the rain will keep off for the braavleis," said Mom, in her visiting voice, and looked hard at me, and I had to get up and go inside with her. But I could see Greg didn't want us to go at all, and I could see Moy knew it. Her eyes were blue again, a pale thin blue, and her mouth was small.

Well, Mom went into the kitchen, and I went into our bedroom, because I could see what went on on the veranda from behind the curtains.

Greg sat on the veranda wall, and whistled »I love you, yes I do.« Suddenly Moira got down off the wall, and stretched herself like a cat. Then he said, "You'd better not wear that dress to the braavleis, it's going to rain."

Moira didn't say a word for what seemed about half an hour, and then she said, in that lazy sort of voice, "Well, Greg Jackson, if you've changed your mind it's okay with me."

"Changed my mind?" he said, very quick, and he looked scared, and she looked scared, and she asked, "What did you say all those things for last night?"

"Say what?" he asked, more scared than ever, and I could see he was trying to remember what he'd said.

Moira was just looking at him. I wouldn't have liked

86

to be Greg Jackson just then, I can tell you. Then she walked off the veranda, through the kitchen, into our room, and sat on the bed.

"I'm not going to the braavleis, Mom," she said, in that sweet slow voice like Mom when she's got visitors and she wishes they'd go.

Mom just sighed, and Dad said half aloud, "Oh my God preserve me!"

Then Mom went on to the veranda. Greg was still sitting there looking sick. "Well, son," Mom said, in her easy voice, the voice she had when she was tired of everything, but keeping up, "Well, son, I think Moy's got a bit of headache from the heat."

I wasn't sweet on Greg those holidays but if I was Moy I would have been, the way he looked just then, all sad but grown up, like a man, when he said, "Mrs Hughes, I don't know what I've done." Mom just smiled, and sighed. "I can't marry, Mrs Hughes, I've got five years' training ahead of me."

Mom smiled and said, "Of course, son, of course."

I was lying on my bed with my stamps, and Moira was on her bed, listening. "Listen to him," she said, in a loud voice, "M a r r y? Why does everyone go on about marrying? They're crazy. I wouldn't marry Greg Jackson anyway if he was the last man on a desert island."

Outside, I could hear Mom sigh hard, then her voice quick and low, and then the sound of Greg's feet walking along the path.

Then Mom came back into our room, and Moira said, all despairing, "Mom, what made you say that about marrying?"

"He said it, my girl, I didn't."

"Marrying!" said Moira, laughing hard.

Mom said, "What did he s a y then, you talked about him saying something?"

"Oh you all make me sick," said Moira, and lay down on her bed, turning away from us. Mom nodded her head at me, and we went out. By then it was five in the afternoon and the cars would be leaving at six, so Mum packed the food, and then she went across to Jordan's house. Moira did not see her go, because she was still lost to the world in her bed.

Soon Mom came back and put the food into the car. Then Jordan came over with Beth from the store and said to me, "Betty, my Mom says, will you and Moy come in our car to the braavleis, because your car's full of food."

"I will," I said, "but Moira's got a headache."

But at this moment Moira called out from the room. "Thanks, Jordan. I'd like to come."

So Mum called to Dad, and they went off in our car together. Moira and I went with Jordan and Beth in their car. I could see Jordan was angry because he wanted to be with Beth, and Beth kept smiling at Moira with her eyebrows up, to tell her she knew what was going on, and Moira smiled back, and talked a lot in her visiting voice.

The braavleis took place high up at the end of the *vlei,* where it rose into a small hill full of big rocks. The grass had been cut that morning by the farmer who always let us use his farm for the braavleis. It was pretty, with the hill behind and the moon coming up over it, and then the cleared space, and the vlei sweeping down to the river, and the trees on either side. The moon was just over the trees when we got there, so the trees looked black and big. The great bonfire was roaring up twenty feet, and in the space around the fire it was all hot and red. The *trench* of *embers* where the *spits* for the meat were, was on one side, and Moira went

spit

---

*vlei,* in South Africa, a piece of low-lying ground covered with water in the rainy season.
*trench,* a channel cut in the earth.
*ember,* glowing coal or piece of wood.

there as soon as she arrived, and helped with the cooking.

Greg was not there, and I thought he wouldn't come, but much later, when we were all eating the meat, and laughing because it burned our fingers it was so hot, I saw him on the other side of the fire talking to Mom. Moira saw him talking, and she didn't like it, but she pretended not to see.

By then we were seated in a half-circle on the side of the fire the wind was blowing, so that the red flames were sweeping off away from us. There were about fifty people from the station and some farmers from round about. Moira sat by me, quietly eating. She was pleased I was there for once, so that she wouldn't seem to be by herself. She had changed her dress back again. It was the dress she had last year for the braavleis, so it wasn't very modern any more. Across the fire, I could see Greg. He did not look at Moira and she did not look at him. He was sitting on his legs, with his hands on his knees. I could see his legs and knees and his big hands all red from the fire. His face was red too and wet with the heat.

Then everybody began singing. We were singing »Sarie Marais«, and »Sugar Bush«, and »Henrietta's Wedding«, and »We don't want to go home«. Moira and Greg were both singing as hard as they could.

It began to get late. The natives were covering the cooking trench with earth, and looking for bits of meat, and the big fire was sinking down. It would be time in a minute for the big dance in a circle around the fire.

Moira was just sitting. Her legs had got *scratches*

---

*scratch,* a thin wound on the surface of the skin.

from the grass. Her hair, that she had curled yesterday, was tied back in a *ribbon,* so that her face looked small and thin.

I said, "Here, Moy, don't look so sad," and she said, "I will if I like." Then she gave me a bit of a grin, and she said, "Let me give you a word of warning for when you're grown-up, don't believe a word men say, I'm telling you."

But I could see she was feeling better just then.

At that very moment the red light of the fire on the grass just in front of us went out, and someone sat down, and I hoped it was Greg and it was.

"Moy," he said, all quiet and calm, "I want to talk to you."

"My name is Moira," said Moy, looking him in the eyes.

"Oh *heck,* Moira," he said, sounding *exasperated* just like Dad.

I moved back a little from the two of them into the crowd that was still softly singing »Sarie Marais«, and looking at the way the fire was glowing low and soft. I could just hear what they said, I wasn't going to move too far off, I can tell you.

"I don't know what I've said," said Greg.

"It doesn't matter in the slightest," said Moira. "But why did you say that about marrying?" Her voice was trembling. She was going to cry if she didn't watch out.

"I thought you thought I meant . . ."

"You think too much," said Moira. She put up her

---

*ribbon,* a narrow band of silk or other material, used for tying hair etc.
*heck,* hell! (curse).
*exasperated,* angry to the point of despairing.

hand and stroked the long tail of hair lying on her shoulder.

"Moira, I've got another five years at university. I couldn't say to you, let's be *engaged* for five years."

"I never said you should," said Moira, examining the scratches on her legs.

The way she was sitting, curled up sideways, with her hair lying forward on her shoulder, it was pretty, it was as pretty as I've ever seen, and I could see his face, sad and almost sick.

"You're so pretty, Moy," he said.

Moira seemed not to be able to move. Then she turned her head slowly and looked at him. I could see the beginning of something terrible on her face.

"You're so beautiful," he said, sounding angry, leaning right forward with his eyes almost into her face. "When you look like that" he said, "it makes me feel…"

People were getting up now all around us. The fire had burned right down, it was a low wave of red heat coming out at us. The moon had come out again, and the cloud had rolled on. It was funny the way the light was red to their shoulders, with the white of the moon on their faces, and their eyes shining like that. I didn't like it. It was the most peculiar moment of all my life.

"Well," said Moira. She sounded just too tired even to try to understand, "that's what you said last night, wasn't it?"

"Don't you see," he said, trying to explain, his tongue all mixed up, "I can't help – I love you, I don't know . . ."

---

*engaged,* bound by a promise of marriage.

Now she smiled, and I knew the smile at once. It was the way Mom smiled at Dad when if he had any sense he'd shut up. It was sweet and loving, but it was sad, and as if she was saying, Lord, you're a fool, Dickson Hughes!

Moira went on smiling like that at Greg, and he was sick and angry and not understanding a thing.

"I love you," he said again.

"Well I love you and what of it?" said Moira.

"But it will be five years."

"And what has that got to do with anything?" at this she began to laugh.

"But Moy . . ."

"My name is Moira," she said, once and for all.

For a moment they were both white and angry, their eyes shining with the big white moon over them.

There was a shout and a rush, and suddenly all the people were in the big circle around the big low heap of fire. They were dancing around and around, yelling and screaming. Greg and Moira stayed where they were, and they didn't hear a thing.

"You're so pretty," he was saying, in that rough, angry voice. "I love you, Moira. There couldn't be anyone but you."

She was smiling, and he went on saying, "I love you, I see your face all the time, I see your hair and your face and your eyes."

I wished he'd go on, the poor fool, just saying it, for every minute, it was more like last night when I woke up and I thought it had rained. The feeling of the dry earth with the rain just on it, that was how she was. She looked as if she would sit there and listen for ever to the words he said, and she didn't want to hear him say-

94

ing, "Why don't you say something Moy, you don't say anything, you do understand don't you? – it's not fair, it isn't right to bind you when we're so young." But he started on saying it in just a minute, and then she smiled her visiting smile, and said, "Gregory Jackson, you're a fool."

Then she got herself off the grass and went across to Mom to help load the car up. She never once looked at Greg again, not for the rest of the holidays.

## Questions

1. What happened when Moira and Greg first met?

2. How does Moira behave after their first meeting?

3. How do the parents feel about it?

4. Which games does Moira play to get hold of Greg?

5. Why is Greg worried?

6. What means does Moira use to get her way in the end?

7. What goes on at a braavleis?

8. What part does the little sister play in the story?